GEORGE AND MARTHA

TWO GREAT FRIENDS

For George and Cecille

The stories in this book were originally published by
Houghton Mifflin Company in *George and Martha*
Copyright © 1972 by James Marshall
Copyright © renewed 2000 by Sheldon Fogelman

www.houghtonmifflinbooks.com

Library of Congress Cataloging-in-Publication data is on file.
READER ISBN-13: 978-0-618-96178-8
Printed in Singapore

TWP 10 9 8 7 6 5 4 3 2 1

George and Martha

Two Great Friends

written and illustrated by
JAMES MARSHALL

HOUGHTON MIFFLIN
COMPANY BOSTON

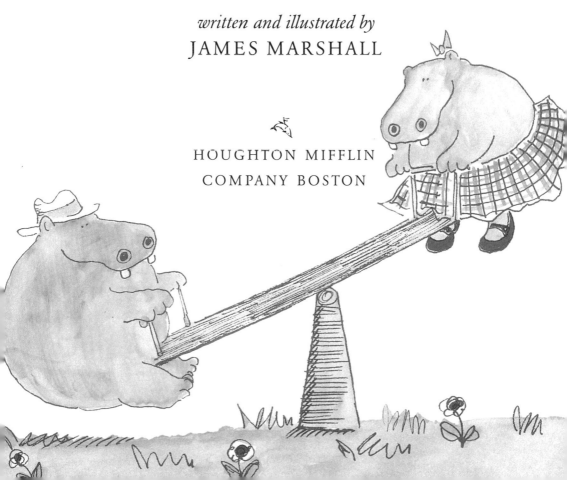

THREE STORIES ABOUT TWO GREAT FRIENDS

The Tub

STORY NUMBER ONE

George was fond of peeking in windows.

One day George peeked in on
Martha.

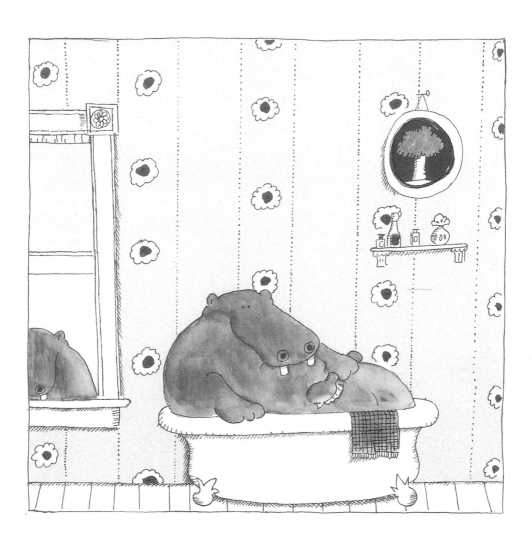

He never did that again.

"We are friends," said Martha. "But there is such a thing as privacy!"

STORY NUMBER TWO

The Mirror

"How I do love to look at myself in the mirror," said Martha. Every chance she got, Martha looked at herself in the mirror.

Sometimes Martha even woke up
during the night to look at herself.
"This is fun." She giggled.

But George was getting tired of watching
Martha look at herself in the mirror.
One day George pasted a silly picture he
had drawn of Martha onto the mirror.
What a scare it gave Martha. "Oh dear!"
she cried. "What has happened to me?"
"That's what happens when you look at
yourself too much in the mirror,"
said George.
"Then I won't do it ever again,"
said Martha.
And she didn't.

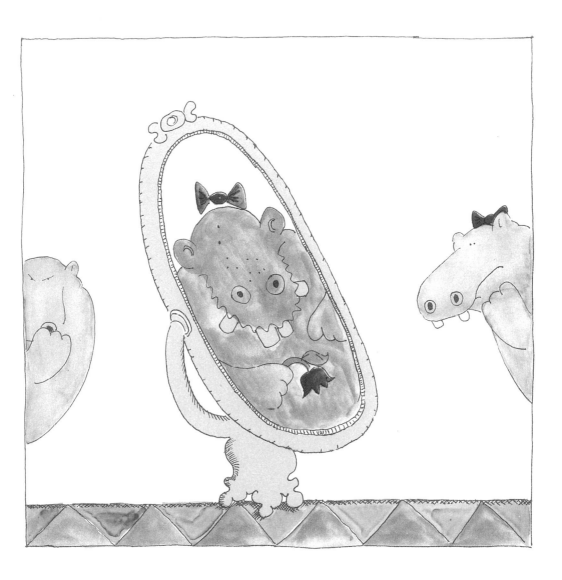

19

THE LAST STORY

STORY

The Tooth

One day when George was skating to
Martha's house, he tripped and fell.
And he broke off his right front tooth.
His favorite tooth too.

When he got to Martha's, George cried his eyes out. "Oh dear me!" he cried. "I look so funny without my favorite tooth!"

"There, there," said Martha.

The next day George went to the dentist.
The dentist replaced George's missing
tooth with a lovely gold one.

When Martha saw George's lovely new golden tooth, she was very happy.

"George!" she exclaimed. "You look so handsome and distinguished with your new tooth!"

And George was happy too. "That's what friends are for," he said. "They always look on the bright side and they always know how to cheer you up."

"But they also tell you the truth," said Martha with a smile.

JAMES MARSHALL (1942–1992)
is one of the most popular and celebrated
artists in the field of children's literature.
Three of his books were selected as New
York Times Best Illustrated Books, and he
received a Caldecott Honor Award in 1989
for *Goldilocks and the Three Bears*. With more
than seventy-five books to his credit, includ-
ing the popular George and Martha series,
Marshall has earned the admiration and
love of countless readers.